Crazy Little Shadow

Virginia LeBlanc Baker
and
Dana LeBlanc Corvino

ISBN 978-1-0980-6722-9 (paperback)
ISBN 978-1-0980-8289-5 (hardcover)
ISBN 978-1-0980-6723-6 (digital)

Christian Faith Publishing, Inc.
832 Park Avenue
Meadville, PA 16335
www.christianfaithpublishing.com

Printed in the United States of America

I, Grandma Baker, dedicate "Crazy Little Shadow" to my wonderful grandchildren and great grandchildren whom I love dearly! "May the LORD bless them and protect them. May the LORD smile on them and be gracious to them. May the LORD show them his favor and give them his peace." Numbers 6:24–26 (NLT Paraphrased)

Credits: "Baby Shark" is a nursery
song about a shark family.

A dance version of "Baby Shark" was popularized online in the 2007 YouTube video "Kleiner Hai" (German for Little Shark) and published by Alexandra Müller, also known by her stage name Alemuel. The video quickly gained popularity and EMI offered Alemuel a record deal and published the song on May 30, 2008. The single peaked at 25th on the German charts and at 21 in the Austrian charts. Based on the single and the original video, the YouTube community created a popular music video. The German version of the song remains popular among German youth groups and multiple variations have been published.

The "Baby Shark" song was further popularized by a video produced by Pinkfong, an education brand within South Korean media startup SmartStudy. The original video for "Baby Shark" was uploaded on November 26, 2015. All videos related to Pinkfong's song have garnered around five billion views as of January 2019, making it the most-viewed educational video phenomenon of all time.

As of July 2020, the most popular video of the "Baby Shark" song (labeled as "Baby Shark Dance"), uploaded on June 17, 2016, has received over six billion views worldwide, making it the second most-viewed video on YouTube.

"BABY SHARK" TRACK INFO

Written by: Robin Davies and Shawnee Lamb

Release date: June 17, 2016

Baby Shark (R&B Remix) by Desmond Dennis

In 2019, it was announced that "Baby Shark" would be adapted into a Nickelodeon series set to premiere on Nickelodeon's Nick Jr. block and the Nick Jr. channel in 2020.

"One more big swing, Colette!" shouted Daddy Baker as he yanked the cowboy boot piñata up and down! Colette's best friends, D'Ion and Isabella, were screaming excitedly, "Come on, Colette. We want to see what's inside!"

Adriel, Colette's two-year-old little sister, was joyfully bouncing up and down on her spring rocking horse when all the sudden, "Kaboom!" Colette whacked the piñata; it broke open, and candy and toys spilled out everywhere!

"Yay!" Colette and her friends cheered at full volume and scurried to get some piñata goodies. Right at that moment, Mommy Baker stepped out on their sunny back patio with a candlelit "Horsie" birthday cake and shouted, "Happy four-year-old birthday, my little cowgirl. Time for cake!"

While Colette and her friends were still yelling enthusiastically, they gathered around the decorated picnic table. Daddy Baker walked over to get Adriel and noticed something funny; Adriel's eyes were focused on the goodies that spilled out under the piñata, but her head was moving back and forth and back and forth as if she was watching a rolling ball.

Daddy Baker picked her up and set her under the piñata. With her eyes focused, her head continued moving side to side, and then she reached out like she was going to grab a toy but instead slapped at a moving shadow.

He watched for a moment and then burst out laughing! He called out to the rest, "Hey, everyone, Adriel's trying to catch a shadow!"

Colette and her friends came running over and eagerly tried catching it with Adriel.

4

Daddy Baker got a good idea and stopped the piñata from swinging.

"We did it!" D'lon yelled. "We caught the shadow!"

He began jumping up and down while his shadow followed, and the others joined in.

"Hahaha!" Isabella laughed. "Our shadows are dancing!"

Mommy Baker joined the fun, "Okay, you triplets, let's all dance over to the table so we can have some yummy birthday cake!"

Daddy Baker placed Adriel on his lap and said, "Would you kids like to hear a poem Mommy Baker wrote many years ago about a crazy little shadow?"

They all clapped and shouted, "Yes! Yes! Yes!"

"Okay!" Mommy Baker replied. "Here it is."

Crazy little shadow, following me around,

What do you think you're trying to see?

Perhaps you think you're smart, but I knew

it from the start that you're trying to be exactly

like me.

Crazy little shadow, why don't you run and play

With other little shadows all around?

You would if it would please, but you'd rather

stay and tease me by hanging out without a word

or sound.

No matter what I do each day, whether it's

work or play,

You come along and imitate each thing I do

and say,

But…crazy little shadow, I'd miss you if you'd go.

You're a good pal to stick around so long.

I know the sun is out, whenever your about,

And when that is true, then nothing can go

wrong.

"That's my poem," declared Mommy Baker.

"I really like that poem," Daddy Baker said and started clapping his hands energetically.

The kids agreed and started clapping also, but then, Isabella appeared curious and posed a question, "Why do shadows follow us?"

Daddy Baker smiled and said, "Well, Isabella, a shadow is just a dark shape that appears when something comes between rays of light and a surface. Stick out your hands over the picnic table. See, our hands created a shadow because they came between the bright sunlight and the picnic table. Now move your fingers around, and your shadows will imitate every move you make."

The kids giggled and moved their hands about.

"Hey," Daddy Baker said, "why don't we have a surprise shadow show when your parents get here? We can show them what you learned today."

"Yay!" they all yelled happily.

Daddy Baker got busy and strung up a dark-red sheet in their living room to represent a stage curtain, and he took down all the pictures so they would have a smooth wall surface for the show.

While Mommy Baker was putting Adriel down for her nap, she got an idea.

"Hey, Colette, D'lon, and Isabella, how about we perform 'Baby Shark'?"

"Yay!" the kids shouted and started singing, "Baby shark doo, doo, doo, doo, doo, doo. / Baby shark doo, doo, doo, doo, doo, doo. / Baby shark doo, doo, doo, doo, doo, doo, baby shark!"

Mommy Baker chuckled. "Well, I guess that's a yes."

So, Mommy Baker got six sheets of poster board. She drew the outlines of a small baby shark on poster board one, the outline of a medium mommy shark on poster board; two, another medium grandma shark on poster board three, the outline of a large daddy shark on poster board; four, an extra-large grandpa shark on poster board five, and several different shaped fish on poster board six! She then carefully cut out the shark family and grouping of fish. She also sketched and cut out larger sharks so the kids could decorate the cutouts with gel crayons, glue, and sparkles.

"They twinkle!" Colette said.

"They sure do," Mommy Baker replied. "You all did a nice job decorating them."

"Yeah," Isabella agreed. "They're so colorful and bright!"

"Okay," Mommy Baker instructed, "we have to let them dry so Daddy Baker can hang them by the front door. Then when your parents get here, our glittery shark family will greet them!"

Colette, D'lon, and Isabella cheered loudly and started singing again, "Baby shark doo, doo, doo, doo, doo doo..."

Mommy Baker butt in and said, "You are right. It's time to rehearse." She held up one of the shark templates. "Look, there is a shark hole where the shark was cut out."

"Oh," Colette said, "I see it, Mommy."

"We do too," D'lon and Isabella agreed.

"Well," Mommy Baker continued, "we're going to use this part to create our shark show."

Mommy Baker handed out the shark and fish templates. Colette got the baby shark, Isabella got the mommy shark, D'lon got the daddy shark, Mommy Baker got the grandma shark, and Daddy Baker got the grandpa shark and all the fishes. Mommy Baker turned on the music and turned out the lights.

Daddy Baker had some bright flashlights and showed Colette, D'lon, and Isabella how to hold them behind their shark templates so their sharks would light up on the wall surface.

"Look, Mommy," Colette said, "our sharks are swimming on the wall!"

"Yay!" they all cheered.

"This is fun!" Isabella shouted.

They rehearsed for a while, and then the doorbell chimed! Colette, D'lon, and Isabella ran excitedly and hid behind the stage curtain and giggled with glee. Mommy Baker invited D'lon and Isabella's parents to come inside. Their heads almost bumped right into the brightly colored sharks hanging from the ceiling.

"Wow," Daddy Rodriguez said with a smile. "What a nice-looking shark family!"

The other daddy and mommies joyfully agreed.
"Well," Mommy Baker said, "we have a surprise for you! Today, our kids learned how shadows form when something comes between rays of light and a surface, and they have worked really hard so they can put on a show for you!"

"Well," Mommy Jordan responded, "I guess we need to come in and sit down then because I love a good show!"

The other parents chuckled and agreed.

When they were all seated comfortably, Daddy Baker enthusiastically thrust open the curtain and said, "Ladies and gentlemen, our kids, with the help of Mommy Baker and I, are going to perform an exciting shadow show called, *Baby Shark's Adventure*!"

The music began playing as the performers made their sharks swim joyfully across the wall. "Baby shark doo, doo, doo, doo, doo, doo. / Mommy shark doo, doo, doo, doo, doo, doo. / Daddy shark doo, doo, doo, doo, doo, doo. / Grandma shark doo, doo, doo, doo, doo, doo. / Grandpa shark doo, doo, doo, doo, doo, doo..." And then the shark family, from baby shark to grandpa shark, decided it was time for a snack, so they went hunting for a school of fish.

When they saw some yummy fish swimming ahead of them, the chase was on, and they swam quickly across the wall to the right and then they swam quickly across the wall to the left!

"Go, little fish!" Daddy Jordan yelled.

The other parents joined in, "Hurry, don't let them catch you!"

And then lo and behold, the little fish hid and got away. The audience yelled, "Yay!"

When the music ended and the lights came on, the kids giggled and said, "I guess they will have to eat a seaweed salad instead. The end!"

"Bravo! Hooray!" D'lon and Isabella's parents joyously applauded. Colette's birthday party was a huge success, and everyone left with big smiles on their faces.

At bedtime, Colette asked her mommy and daddy, "Can I have a shadow show again?"

"Absolutely!" they replied. "I also liked your poem, Mommy. I would like to write a poem too!" Colette added.

"Sure," Mommy Baker agreed. "Since it's still your birthday, how about we write a short one right now?"

"Yay!" Colette yelled.

And this is what they wrote:

God's children are all colors, how wonderful how fun!

But their shadows are the same when they're under the sun.

With sleepy eyes, Colette said her prayers and whispered, "Good night, Mommy and Daddy. I love you!"

"Good night, sweetheart. We love you too!" they replied. "Maybe tomorrow, you can plan another shadow show!"

And she did!

Okay, now it's your turn to write a poem and create a shadow show on your wall. Have fun!

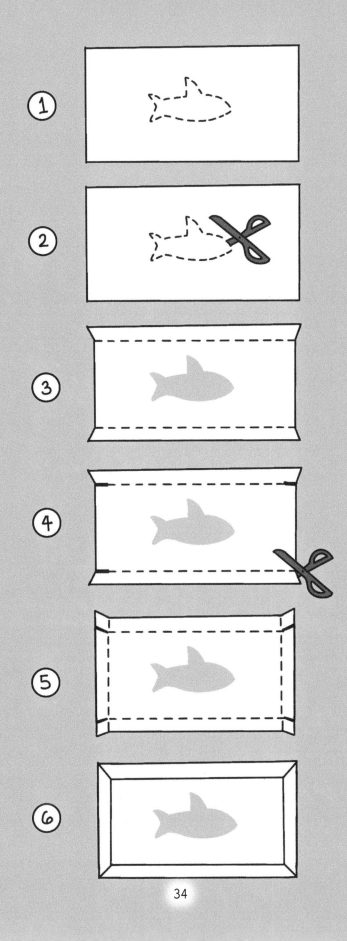

About the Author

Ninety-four-year-old Virginia LeBlanc Baker has three daughters, one stepdaughter, one stepson, ten grandchildren, and seven great-grandchildren and counting. For decades, Virginia has been writing songs, poetry, and short stories. Her poem "Crazy Little Shadow" inspired this book. This will be  her first published work with her youngest daughter, Dana LeBlanc Corvino. She has always loved teaching children and hopes to send a positive message to all who love to read during their story hour.

CPSIA information can be obtained
at www.ICGtesting.com
Printed in the USA
JSHW011923290421
14154JS00002B/5

9 781098 067229